The Werewolf in the Living Room

Look for more books in the Goosebumps Series 2000
by R.L. Stine:

The Werewolf in the Living Room

AN
APPLE
PAPERBACK

SCHOLASTIC INC.
New York Toronto London Auckland Sydney
Mexico City New Delhi Hong Kong

A PARACHUTE PRESS BOOK

No part of this publication may be reproduced in whole or in part, or stored in a retrieval system, or transmitted in any form or by any means, electronic, mechanical, photocopying, recording, or otherwise, without written permission of the publisher. For information regarding permission, write to Scholastic Inc., Attention: Permissions Department, 555 Broadway, New York, NY 10012.

ISBN 0-590-68521-X

Copyright © 1999 by Parachute Press, Inc.
All rights reserved. Published by Scholastic Inc.
APPLE PAPERBACKS, SCHOLASTIC, and associated logos are
trademarks and/or registered trademarks of Scholastic Inc.
GOOSEBUMPS is a registered trademark
of Parachute Press, Inc.

12 11 10 9 8 7 6 5 4 3 2 1   9/9 0 1 2 3 4/0

Printed in the U.S.A.   40

First Scholastic printing, May 1999

Part One

"**A**aron, would you be quiet, please?" Dad stepped lightly, weaving his way between the trees. "Try not to walk like an elephant. We don't want them to hear us coming."

I *was* walking like an elephant. Stomping through the dark, chilly forest. Stomping hard on the last brittle leaves of winter. Making the leaves crunch and crackle as loudly as I could.

I wanted THEM to hear us coming. I wanted to scare THEM away.

THEM.

WEREWOLVES.

It was close to midnight as we crept through the woods. Dark woods where the trees grew thick and close together. Woods where a werewolf could easily hide. Where a werewolf could leap out of the

3

shadows before you knew it. Lunge for your neck. Sink his teeth deep into your skin — and pierce your throat.

I pictured blood spurting from a hole in my neck. I shuddered.

Back home, I didn't know if I believed in werewolves or not. Here in the dark forest ... I was starting to believe.

Why was I in the forest hunting werewolves? Let me explain.

I — Aaron Freidus — am eleven years old. I have curly red hair, freckles, and light green eyes. I'm tall and skinny. I mean really skinny. Mom used to say I was so skinny a breeze could blow me over.

Mom died two years ago. I live with my dad, which wouldn't be bad — except for one thing. My dad is weird. Really. He doesn't do any of the normal things a dad is supposed to do. You know, go to baseball games in the spring. Barbecue hot dogs in the summer. Shovel snow in the winter.

Why?

Because I — Aaron Freidus — have a dad who is a werewolf hunter.

Dad's big dream in life is to catch a real werewolf.

Every chance he gets, he prowls the woods outside our town, hunting werewolves.

He hasn't found one yet.

My friends know about my dad and his were-wolf hunting. But they don't make fun of him. They're afraid to. That's because Dad is tall and powerful looking, with shoulders wider than a football player's. *And* he's the sheriff of our town.

No, my friends don't make fun of my dad. They're not that stupid. Instead, they make fun of *me*.

That's why I had to lie about our midterm break. I told everyone we were going to Florida to visit my grandmother.

But we weren't going to Florida. We were going to Bratvia. A country I never heard of, in the middle of Europe.

Bratvia. Dad couldn't wait to go there — to hunt werewolves.

I couldn't wait to go there — so I could come home again!

Dad thinks Bratvia is crawling with were-wolves.

What do I think?

Do werewolves exist — or is my dad crazy?

I was about to find out. . . .

An icy breeze blew hard through the dark forest. I stopped and listened. Listened to the animal cries the wind carried with it.

Mournful wails. Angry caws. Fierce screeches.

And howls. Hungry howls. The howls scared me the most.

I glanced up at the night sky — at the bright full moon that hung there. It bathed the treetops in an eerie silver glow.

Werewolves come out during a full moon, I remembered, and eat people.

I shuddered again.

I tried to remember everything I had read about werewolves. In some stories, humans turned into werewolves by putting on wolf skins. Or by drinking water from a wolf's paw print.

What else did I know?

Oh, right — how could I forget the most important stuff?

You could force a werewolf to change back to human form by shouting out the werewolf's real name. Or by knocking on the creature's forehead three times.

That's it.

That's all I knew about werewolves.

"Aaron, don't just stand there!" Dad turned around and whispered. "You're a perfect target. You want to be the hunter — not the *hunted*!"

"Okay, okay, Dad. I'm coming." I began tiptoeing through the dead leaves.

Dad picked up the pace, moving skillfully and swiftly — like an animal that has caught the scent of its prey.

"Dad, slow down!" I called, panic creeping into my voice. "It's too dark. I'm going to lose you."

But my father didn't slow down. He moved faster. Trotting now.

"Dad, please! Slow down!" I yelled, breaking into a run.

Why won't he wait for me? I wondered, running faster. Gasping for breath.

"Dad! Wait! I can't keep up!"

My sides ached. I couldn't see where I was going. I stumbled over the root of a tree. Scraped my face against its trunk. Felt a trickle of blood run down my face.

I ran faster.

But the faster I ran, the faster Dad ran.

"Dad!" I finally shouted. "STOP!"

Dad stopped.

He whirled around to face me — and I screamed.

2

Thick brown fur sprouted from my father's face. I watched in horror as his nose lengthened into a snout. He curled back his lips — and sharp fangs slipped from his gums.

He stood with his legs wide apart. He heaved his chest forward. Then threw back his head — and howled at the moon.

I tried to scream. I tried to run. But I couldn't move. I could only gape in terror.

Totally covered in fur now, Dad dropped down on all fours.

He gazed hard at me with gleaming black eyes.

From the back of his throat he let out a low, menacing snarl.

"This is a dream," I whispered. "Please. This has to be a dream.

"Only a dream," I turned in my bed, murmuring. "Only a dream."

Yes! It *was* only a dream.

Still half asleep, I brushed my hair back off my forehead. It was wet and matted with sweat. I turned my pillow over. It felt cool against my hot cheeks.

"Only a dream," I murmured. It felt so good to wake up from it.

I closed my eyes and drifted off to sleep again. . . .

And started another dream . . .

Now I was lying on a cot in a tent, with rain beating hard on the tent walls.

I covered my ears. I tried to shut out the pounding rain. The rain stopped.

But now I heard another sound.

Clawing. Something clawing the tent wall. Something trying to get in!

I held my breath and listened closely. The clawing grew louder, more frantic.

I bolted up in my bed.

No, not my bed.

I *am* on a cot. I *am* in a tent, I realized. A tent in the middle of the forest.

I'm not dreaming anymore!

This is real!

I stared at the tent wall.

My heart raced as it shook violently. As the clawing grew wilder.

And then I let out a gasp — as the tent wall split open with a sharp *RIIIIP*.

9

leaped out of bed.

I bolted across the tent. Then stopped. I was too frightened to see what was clawing its way into my tent.

"Please go away," I wished. "Whatever you are — leave." I closed my eyes and wished harder. "Leave so I can go back to sleep and get up in the morning, when it's light outside — and safe."

More clawing. Rougher. More savage.

My legs began to tremble.

"Calm down, Aaron," I told myself. "Just look outside. You'll see, there's nothing to fear. It's probably just a raccoon out there."

I wiped my sweaty palms on my navy-blue T-shirt. My hands shook as I gently opened the tent flap.

I took a deep breath.

I peeked outside.

Nothing there now.

Whatever had ripped my tent was gone.

I stared out at the trees, tall and black against the dark sky. Dad and I entered this creepy forest three days ago. And every night since then I've had terrifying werewolf dreams.

Is there really a werewolf hiding in this forest? I wondered.

I opened the tent flap a little wider. Stretched my head out. Gazed around the small clearing.

In front of my tent, the remains of our evening campfire still smoldered. I watched a white ribbon of smoke rise and disappear in the breeze.

I glanced to the right — at Dad's tent.

No movement there.

No clawing sounds.

I stepped outside.

Except for the soft rustling of the trees, the forest was quiet. The air felt crisp against my skin. I shivered as I looked up at the full moon.

I wandered a little farther from my tent.

I listened for night sounds — the hoot of an animal, the grunt of a bear. But I didn't hear anything.

Nothing but an eerie silence.

My heart began to pound again.

Dad said there were two good reasons to go on this trip.

The first reason: to catch a werewolf.

The second reason: to toughen me up. I guess Dad thought a sheriff shouldn't have a wimp for a son.

Well, Dad hasn't caught a werewolf. And I'm more afraid than ever. Two good reasons to leave, I thought.

I stared up at the moon again — and remembered something else Dad told me.

"Don't go out by yourself," he warned me when we arrived. "The townspeople swear a werewolf prowls this forest. And there will be a full moon while we're here. That means the werewolf *will* be out. And he'll be hunting for fresh meat."

Dad and the townspeople sounded so sure of themselves. So certain that werewolves were real. That one stalked this forest.

My heart hammered in my chest now.

I turned to my tent — but I was too scared to sleep by myself.

I'll sleep in Dad's tent tonight. I'll tell him I have a stomachache so he doesn't think I'm scared.

I made my way over to his tent.

I quietly lifted the flap.

I peered inside. "Dad?"

He was gone.

I heard a crackling noise behind me. I whirled around and listened.

Footsteps, I thought. Heavy feet crunching over leaves on the forest floor.

"That must be Dad!" I assured myself. "I'll go find him. I don't want to stay here by myself."

I raced to my tent. I fumbled in the dark for my jeans and sneakers. I quickly slipped them on and ran back outside.

I could still hear the crackling leaves. "Good," I said. "He's nearby."

I left the small clearing and headed down a narrow path in the woods. The silvery moon lit my way.

"Hey, Dad!" I started to call out to him, but stopped.

"That was really stupid." I shook my head.

"Why don't you let every bear in the forest know where you are?"

But it wasn't the bears I was worried about.

I tried to follow the sound of the footsteps. I listened hard. But I couldn't tell exactly where they were coming from. I reached a fork in the path. Should I keep walking straight ahead? I wondered. Should I take the turn? I didn't know what to do. As I stood there, trying to decide, the footsteps grew quieter. More distant.

I took the turn and started to run. Following the faint sounds, I raced deeper into the forest. The trees grew closer together here. Their tops formed a dark curtain against the sky. Against the light of the moon.

I ran in total darkness. Stumbling. Crashing into trees. "Why did you have to leave our campsite, Dad?" I wailed.

I stopped to listen for the footsteps — but the woods were totally silent.

Why are these woods so quiet? I shuddered. *So unreal.*

And then I heard the sharp snap of a twig.

That must be Dad!

I took off. I followed the path as it twisted and turned. Dodged low branches. Dodged the mossy water that dripped from their leaves.

I stopped to catch my breath.

I'm never going to find him! It's too dark. I don't know where I'm going!

"Dad! Dad! Where are you?" I shouted.

I heard another snap of a twig — this time over my head.

I froze.

I heard a low snarl. Then the sharp crack of a tree branch.

I glanced up — and stared into glowing black eyes.

An animal?

What *was* it?

I didn't have time to see.

I staggered back as it leaped down from the tree branch.

I opened my mouth to scream — but no sound came out!

Half wolf, half human, it stood on all fours. Its bristly fur glistened in the moonlight.

Snarling, drooling, it lumbered up to me.

I gasped in horror. Staggered back.

The creature had the face of a wolf. And the broad back and chest of a man.

He stared at me with those gleaming black eyes. He curled back his thick lips. I stared in horror at long, curved fangs.

Then — before I could run — the werewolf leaned back on his haunches.

Raised his head in a fierce howl.

Leaped hard. Leaped to my shoulder.

And sank his fangs deep into my skin.

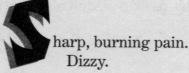harp, burning pain.
Dizzy.

Can't see.

Falling into darkness.

Falling . . . falling . . .

Warm breath on my neck.

He's here. He's back.

"Get away. NOOOOO! DAD! HELP!"

A hand on my shoulder. No — not a hand. A wolf paw!

"NOOOOO! HELP!"

"Aaron, I'm here. It's okay. Calm down."

My eyes flew open. Dad sat on the edge of my cot. He leaned over me, with one hand on my shoulder.

"Aaron, are you okay?" His brow creased with worry.

I sat up. I was lying on my cot. Back in the safety of my tent.

Wait. Did I leave my tent tonight?

I felt so confused.

The race through the woods — the werewolf — was it another nightmare?

I turned to face my dad and felt a throbbing pain in my shoulder.

No. Not a nightmare. This werewolf was real.

"How did I get back here?" I asked.

"I carried you," he answered. "I saw the creature standing over you! I chased him away!" Dad's face flushed with excitement.

"Are you sure he's gone?" I fell back on my pillow.

"Yes. He's gone. He won't be back tonight. But don't worry." Dad jumped and began pacing the tent.

If the creature was gone, why would I worry? I wondered. "What do you mean?" I asked, sitting up again.

"Don't worry," he repeated. "He's gone. But we'll hunt him down tomorrow."

"I don't want to hunt him down tomorrow!" I shouted. "I want to go home tomorrow!"

"This is so thrilling," Dad continued pacing. He hadn't heard a word I said. "We're actually going to capture a werewolf!"

"It's too dangerous, Dad!" I shouted.

Dad stopped pacing. He turned to me, his face filled with confusion. "Dangerous?" He shook his head. "Werewolves have no special strength during the day, Aaron. They are humans like us. It's not dangerous at all."

I could see I wasn't going to win this argument.

"Dad — where did you go?" I asked. "I looked for you in your tent, but you weren't there."

"I couldn't sleep. Too excited to be here, I guess. I went out for a short walk. Thought maybe I'd catch sight of the werewolf. You know how long I've dreamed of capturing one."

Dad opened the flap to my tent and stepped outside. "Good night, Aaron. You're okay. You're okay, son. Get some rest. Tomorrow is the day. Tomorrow is the day we will never forget!" The tent flap closed behind him.

I fell back on my cot.

I pulled my blanket up to my chin.

A strong wind blew the tent flap open.

I wish this tent had a door so I could lock it, I thought, staring at the swaying flap.

I wish I really was in Florida visiting Grandma. I closed my eyes.

I wish I was home, playing baseball with my friends. I started to feel sleepy.

I wish midterm break would be over.

I fell asleep wishing about all the places I'd rather be than here.

I tossed and turned — and drifted into a dream.

Running . . . I was running through the dark, chilly forest.

Running beneath low branches.

Running under a full moon. Running on all fours.

The leaves on the ground brushed against my fur. The smell of the damp earth stung my nostrils. I was running with a pack of wolves. Panting.

NO! I want this dream to stop!

I forced myself awake.

I forced my eyes open and gasped for air.

"It was just a dream," I told myself, trying to slow my breathing. "Another one of those horrible nightmares."

The tent was dark.

It's still night, I realized.

I sat up in bed — and gasped.

At the foot of my bed two black, gleaming eyes stared at me — the eyes of the werewolf!

"Don't hurt me." My voice escaped in a choked whisper.

The werewolf didn't move.

Panting loudly, panting like an animal, he stared at me with those glowing black eyes. His gaze seemed to hold me in a trance.

My heart raced. I was too frightened to sit up. I could only stare back.

Scream, Aaron, SCREAM!

"DAAAAAD!" the word exploded from my throat. "DAAAAD!"

The werewolf's head jerked back. He lifted a paw. Tossed something onto my cot. Then bolted out.

"DAAAAD!"

"Aaron, what's wrong?" I heard Dad call from his tent. "I'll be right there."

I jumped out of bed so fast I flipped the cot over. It crashed into the tent wall, nearly bringing the whole tent down.

"Whoa." Dad stepped into the tent. He raised his arms to steady the wobbly structure. "Aaron, what's wrong? What happened? Why were you screaming?"

"He — he came back, Dad!" I stammered. "He was here. Right here in this tent. Right there." I pointed to the place where the werewolf had stood.

"He came back!" Dad couldn't believe it. "I'm going after him!" He turned to leave. "Oh." He glanced over his shoulder. "Are you okay?"

I started to nod. "I guess. I —"

Dad was gone before I finished.

I picked up my cot and straightened it out. Still shaking, I sat down. "I don't get it. Why did the werewolf come back?" I wondered.

I pictured him standing at the foot of my cot.

Dad said the creature wouldn't be back tonight. But Dad was wrong.

"Dad?"

Is he okay? I wondered.

Maybe he needs my help!

What if something horrible happens to him out there?

What if the werewolf is waiting for him out there?

21

"I should have gone with him!" I leaped out of my cot. "He shouldn't have left me here alone. He should have taken me with him!"

I started to race outside — but something on the floor caught my eye. Something small, white, and sparkling in the corner of the tent.

"What *is* this?" I picked it up and studied it.

Some kind of animal tooth? It was strung like a pendant on a string. I turned it around in my hands, examining it from every angle.

"Where did this come from?"

The werewolf! Yes. Now I remembered him tossing it onto my cot.

I held the pendant up by its string. I stared at it. It was definitely a tooth.

I have to find Dad. I have to show this to him. Maybe it means something.

I charged out of the tent — and gasped. Dad stood right outside the opening.

"I — I didn't know you were out here," I murmured.

"I couldn't find the creature." Dad frowned. "We'll try again tomorrow."

"Look." I held up the pendant. "The werewolf threw this in the tent. Is it a wolf tooth?"

Dad took the pendant. "How strange," he said, studying it. "Why would the werewolf give this to you?"

"What do you think it means, Dad?"

My father shook his head. "I don't really know.

22

But maybe it will bring us good luck on our were-wolf hunt tomorrow." Dad's eyes lit up at the thought. "I think you should wear it."

He slipped the tooth pendant around my neck. As it fell against my chest, I shivered.

And felt a stab of cold — cold dread that spread over my chest until I hugged myself to stop shivering.

"Aaron! Aaron! Come quick!" I woke up the next morning to Dad's frantic cries.

I pulled myself off my cot.

"Hurry! Before it's too late!" His voice sounded shrill and excited. "HURRY! You'll miss it!"

raced out of the tent.

I gazed frantically around our campsite. Nothing there.

No werewolf. Only Dad, wearing a navy-blue baseball cap, jeans, and his favorite red T-shirt. Leaning over an open fire. Frying eggs in a heavy metal skillet.

"What's wrong, Dad?" I cried, my heart pounding. "Too late for what?"

"Too late for breakfast. Don't want your eggs to turn cold." He laughed.

"Not funny," I grumbled.

Dad scraped the eggs from the pan onto the two plates. He handed one to me. "Don't be so grumpy, Aaron. Today is going to be our lucky day. Today we are going to catch a werewolf!"

Today we are going to catch a werewolf. A big lump formed in my throat.

I shoveled some eggs onto my fork. I placed them in my mouth. But I couldn't swallow them. When Dad poured coffee into his cup, I spit the eggs back onto my plate.

"Are you sure it's safe?" I asked. "You know — to try to trap one, I mean?"

"What kind of question is that?" Dad demanded. "That's what we're here for, isn't it?"

"But maybe it's not safe," I repeated. "Maybe werewolves have powers during the day that you don't know about."

"They don't," Dad declared.

"But how do you know?" I asked. "I mean, how can you be so sure?"

My dad knows everything. He knows how to fix a car, a leaky faucet — anything. He knows all about the constellations. He knows when I'm getting sick — before I know it. He even knows how to knit a sweater.

He'll tell me exactly how he knows werewolves don't have powers during the day. Then I'll feel better.

"How do you know that werewolves have no power during the day?" I asked again.

"I don't know how I know." Dad shrugged his shoulders. "I just know."

I didn't feel better.

After breakfast, Dad announced that it was time to break camp. Time to catch a werewolf.

We rolled up our tents, packed all our stuff into two big green backpacks, and headed deeper into the woods.

"How do you know which way to go?" I asked.

"Easy. We just follow these prints." Dad pointed to deep prints in the dirt.

I stared at the prints and shuddered.

We made our way through the woods. The dense treetops blocked out the sun. It's so gloomy here, I thought, stopping to adjust my backpack.

"Dad! Slow down!" I called as I shifted the backpack's weight on my shoulders. But he didn't slow down. He marched quickly, with a spring in his step, eager to catch his prey.

As I caught up to him, he came to an abrupt stop.

"This is it!" he whispered. "I see him!" His eyes grew wide with excitement. Then he took off, running along the twisting, turning path.

My heart pounding, I raced after him.

Dad ran faster, winding his way through the trees.

Up ahead, I spotted a flash of color. A flash of brown fur.

I stopped again.

"There he is." Dad stared at the creature that stood before him. "Just a fox."

A small brown fox gazed at us with frightened eyes. Dad shook his head with disappointment.

"I should have known better," he said. "It's morning. The werewolf will be in human form now. Well, I won't make *that* mistake again."

I was glad Dad made that mistake. I prayed he'd keep making mistakes until it was time to go home. I prayed that by now the werewolf was far, far away.

Dad returned to the path and we continued the hunt.

Today, the forest was filled with sounds. And they were sounds I'd never heard before. Strange animal cries and sharp screeches. And a loud snapping sound — like thousands of fingers snapping.

I glanced up — and gasped. The tree branches were filled with inky blackbirds. Hundreds and hundreds of them. Perched side by side. With dark red eyes. And long, sharp beaks that they opened and closed with a hard *SNAP*.

I'd never seen birds like these before.

As I moved through the trees, I kept my eyes on them. I stared into the thousands of red eyes that peered down at me. And listened to the riot of their snapping beaks.

"Are they angry?"

I kept staring up at them.

"Hungry?"

I kept staring up at them.

"I don't want to find out."

I tore my eyes away — and gasped.

The path ahead of me stood empty.

Dad had disappeared from sight.

"Dad, where are you?" I shouted.

No answer.

I cried out for him again. Again.

I ran through the trees, searching for him. But I didn't see him anywhere.

"Why didn't I keep my eyes on the trail?" I moaned.

My eyes darted frantically through the forest.

"How can I tell where I am?" I cried. "All these trees look the same! I'll never find my way out of these woods! And no one will ever be able to find me."

No one, I thought, except the werewolf.

8

"**D**AD! DAD! DAAAAAD!" I tore down the path, screaming for my father.

My shrill cries rang through the forest.

But no reply. No sign of my father.

I was panting hard now. Exhausted. My throat, too sore to shout.

I slowed down to a walk and made my way through the woods in silence.

I peered hard through the trees, searching for my father. Hoping to catch a glimpse of his red shirt. His green backpack.

I tried to stay calm. But every small sound — the rustling of leaves, the snap of a twig, every animal cry — made my heart leap with fear.

As I walked, I realized that the path was slowly

growing wider. The trees, fewer. The sun, brighter.

And then — the forest opened into a clearing.

I stepped into a bright circle of sunshine — and nearly whooped with joy!

A small wooden shack stood in the clearing. White puffs of smoke floated from its chimney. A warm orange light glowed from a window next to the front door.

I tiptoed up to the window and peered inside. Against the far wall, a fire burned in a hearth. In front of the hearth stood a round wooden table with two chairs.

I craned my neck to take in more of the room — and the door flew open with a crash.

I let out a cry of surprise.

In the doorway stood an old woman. She had jet-black hair that hung down to her waist. But it was thin on top, and I could see patches of pink scalp peeking through.

Wrinkled skin clung to her sunken cheeks. She had a long nose — so long, the tip of it nearly touched her dry, cracked lips.

She wore a tattered purple-and-orange dress made of lace. It hung loosely on her thin body, flowing down to her ankles, down to her gnarled, bare toes.

Her earlobes sagged under the weight of her heavy silver hoop earrings. Shiny silver bracelets decorated her arms, from her wrists all the way up to her elbows.

"What do you want?" Her voice was surprisingly strong and sharp. Her blue eyes shockingly bright.

"I — I'm lost," I stammered.

"Come in, then." She turned and disappeared inside the shack.

I followed the old woman. I stepped inside — and gasped as the door banged shut behind me.

"Scared, aren't you?" The old woman nodded her head. "You should be."

I glanced at the door.

"You're not going anywhere," the woman said, as if she could read my thoughts. "Sit down." She dug her fingers into my shoulder and shoved me toward the wooden table.

"It's not safe to be here." The woman's icy stare sent a shiver down my spine.

"Then I'll go!" I jumped up.

"Sit down!" she ordered again. "It's the woods that aren't safe. Why are you wandering this forest alone?" Her voice grew kinder.

"I'm not alone," I said. "I was with my father. But I lost him."

I told the old woman all about my father. About how much he wanted to catch a werewolf.

"I'm sure your father will turn up here, searching for you. Until then, we'll have some tea — and

31

I will tell you the legend of the werewolf your father hunts."

The old woman stood up and set a kettle on the hearth. Then she returned to the table. She ran her knobby fingers through her thin black hair and began her tale.

"These woods weren't always so quiet," she started. "They echoed with the sounds of children's laughter. But that was a long time ago. Before the stranger arrived."

"The stranger?"

"Yes." The old woman nodded sadly. "A tall, burly man. With thick black hair that hung down to his shoulders. And a long dark beard that hid his face. And glistening black eyes. 'Wolf eyes,' the villagers said.

"No one knew where the man came from. He passed right through town. And the villagers were so glad to see him head into the woods — they didn't stop him to ask any questions.

"But they should have, they all agreed later. They should have stopped him. They should have chased him far away." The old woman's voice grew quieter. "Because that's when the terror began."

She sat back in her chair and closed her eyes tightly — as if trying to shut out some unspeakable horror.

"Wh-what happened?" I stammered.

"It was the night of the full moon. A horrible howl echoed through the forest all night long. And we all heard cries of terrifying agony. None of the villagers could sleep.

"As the sun rose, the sounds faded. Whatever had happened — was over. The villagers sighed with relief. But one of them insisted on searching the woods.

"A small group of men volunteered to go. They found the forest floor littered with dead animals, half eaten and bloody. Torn apart at the limbs.

"And they found something else — wolf prints.

"A few brave men hid in the forest the next night. As the moon rose, they saw the stranger leap down from a tree. He gazed up at the moon and howled.

"The men watched in terror as thick fur sprouted from the stranger's body. As his face lengthened to form a snout. As razor-sharp teeth slipped from his gums.

"A rabbit scampered by. The creature snatched it up and ate it whole.

"The men ran from the forest. Ran all the way back to the village.

"They were the lucky ones.

"Later, there were others who traveled into the forest to try to capture the creature. They never made it back." The old woman let out a long, low sigh.

"Only the foolish and the crazy enter these woods now. No one escapes the werewolf unharmed."

"Is it the same werewolf?" I asked. "The stranger with the wolf eyes?"

She shrugged. "Who knows? Who knows how truthful these old legends are . . . ?" the woman's voice trailed off.

"I hope my dad is okay." My eyes darted to the window.

"I'm sure he's fine. It's daylight. No harm will come to him when the sun shines." The old woman reached across the table and took my hand. "Would you like me to tell your fortune?" She smiled.

I held out my hand.

"This is your lifeline." With a gentle touch, her bony finger traveled over one of the lines in my palm.

I leaned forward to get a better look — and the tooth pendant slipped out from under my shirt.

The tooth swung forward — and the old woman screamed in fright. "The sign of the werewolf!" she shrieked. "How did you get that? Get out! Get out of my house!"

Still shrieking, the old woman leaped up from her chair.

She reached into the hearth and pulled out a red-hot poker.

I bolted from my chair and raced out the door.

My heart pounding, I charged through the clearing. I stumbled over a rock and fell to my knees.

The woman hobbled after me, swinging the hot poker in front of her. "The sign of the werewolf! Get out! Get out!" Her shrieks filled the clearing.

I jumped to my feet and dashed into the woods. I couldn't find the trail, but I didn't care.

I darted between trees. Tripped over tree roots. Kept on going.

Why did she say the tooth was the sign of the werewolf?

Why was she so afraid of it?

I ran until her cries grew faint.

I ran blindly — until I couldn't hear her at all.

Then, even though my sides ached, I ran some more.

I finally stopped when I heard low growls behind me. And snapping jaws.

"The werewolf!" I gasped.

I spun around.

And stared at a pack of wild dogs. At least ten of them. Ugly dogs, their fur matted and dirty. Yellow eyes staring menacingly. Slack jaws dripping with saliva.

Growling loudly, they lowered their scrawny heads. Prepared to attack.

They circled me. Circled. Snapping their jaws hungrily.

I dove for a tree. Frantically, I wrapped my arms and legs around the trunk — and scrambled up.

Howling and barking, the dogs rushed the tree. Leaped at it. Clawed at the trunk.

I shimmied up higher.

The dogs leaped higher, heaving themselves against the tree trunk.

I cried out as a dog sank his teeth into my sneaker. He shook his head wildly, pulling me, pulling me down.

I yanked my foot free. It flew out of my sneaker.

Another dog jumped up and tore at my sock.

I kicked my leg hard, shaking off the ferocious creature. I raised my arms to pull myself higher.

"Nooooo!"

I lost my grip.

And fell flat on my back — into the waiting pack of hungry dogs.

10

Startled by my fall, the dogs froze.

Panting hard, heads lowered, they eyed me, waiting to see what I'd do next.

Then, slowly, as if by some secret signal, they began to move forward.

If I tried to get up, they'd dive for me, I knew. And rip me to shreds.

Growling softly, the dogs inched forward.

The werewolf tooth.

The old woman was afraid of the tooth, I thought. Maybe the dogs will be too.

I slowly raised my hand to my neck.

The dogs moved in closer. I could feel their hot, sour breath on my face.

I reached inside my shirt.

My trembling hand wrapped around the string.

The dogs closed in.

I searched for the tooth.

Where is it? Where?

The dogs were snarling viciously now, preparing to attack.

I tugged desperately at the string. Tugged. Tugged.

The tooth was gone.

jerked my head up. Gave the string a hard yank.

The tooth. It had been *under* me.

I grabbed it.

The dogs leaped.

I raised the animal tooth above me.

Yes!

The dogs practically stopped their attack in midair.

They stopped barking. Gaped at the tooth in silence.

Then, with frightened whimpers, they turned away from me. And scooted into the forest, tails between their legs.

"Wow! I can't believe it worked!" I sat up and gazed into the woods. The dogs were gone. Really gone.

"This tooth is powerful!" I grasped it tightly in the palm of my hand. "It saved my life! I'd better take really good care of it!"

Why does it have such power? I wondered.

Maybe Dad can help me figure it out.

I carefully tucked the tooth back under my shirt. Then I stood up, pulled my sneaker back on, and began searching for my father.

I wandered through the woods until I found a trail to follow.

The woods were quiet now. I didn't see those strange blackbirds or hear the *SNAP, SNAP, SNAP* of their beaks.

I didn't see a squirrel or a rabbit.

I didn't see or hear anything.

But I wasn't scared.

I touched the tooth hidden beneath my shirt — and I felt safe.

I don't know how long I walked.

I couldn't tell if I was wandering through a new part of the forest or one I had explored before.

"Dad! Hey — Dad!" I called out for my father as I made my way through the trees.

But Dad didn't answer.

If I don't find him, I'll go crazy! I thought. The calm I had felt before was fading. My pulse started to race.

I walked a little faster.

Shouted a little louder.

"DAAAD! Can you hear me?"

41

No answer.

"DAD! Where are you?"

"Aaron, is that you?" A shout came back.

"Dad! It's me!" I cried. "Where are you?"

"Look up, Aaron. Look for the tallest tree!"

I gazed up. "Okay, Dad, I see it! I'm coming!"

"Hurry, Aaron!" Dad's voice was filled with excitement. "I've got him! I've captured the werewolf!"

I ran as fast as I could. But I really wanted to turn back. I didn't want to see the werewolf. I never wanted to see that creature again.

Through the trees I spotted Dad's red shirt.

I was almost there.

Beads of sweat trailed down my face.

I burst into the clearing — and gasped in shock. "Dad — are you *crazy*?" I cried.

12

"Dad — you're kidding — right?" I
called.

My father leaned against a tree, smiling confidently, staring into the eyes of his prey.

His prey — an ordinary, sad-looking, middle-aged, balding man.

The man stood slightly stooped. He wore a plaid flannel shirt over baggy khakis. His hands were shackled behind his back with a set of Dad's extra-heavy-duty chains. His ankles were bound together with two thick metal cuffs connected by another heavy-duty chain.

This is Dad's werewolf?

I shook my head in disbelief. This guy didn't look as if he could harm a flea.

"Look at him, Dad," I protested. "He's short.

He's pudgy. He wears glasses. He doesn't even have any hair. He can't be a werewolf!"

The little guy nodded sadly — and sneezed.

"And he has a cold! Werewolves don't have colds! Come on, Dad. You have to let him go!"

"Does anyone have a tissue?" The little guy sniffled.

"Here." I reached out to hand him one.

"Aaron — DON'T!" my father screamed — and knocked my hand away. "It could be a trick!"

Dad has really lost it, I thought. This is ridiculous.

The little guy sneezed again.

"Dad, how can you be so sure he's the werewolf?"

"I followed the wolf prints all morning — and they led right to his shack!" Dad exclaimed. "There's no doubt about it. He's the werewolf."

"But he doesn't look like the werewolf!" I shook my head. "Remember, we saw the creature last night. This guy doesn't look anything like him."

"Listen to your son, sir. Please," the little man pleaded. "Let me go."

"Werewolves shed their skin after the full moon has passed." Dad stared hard into the man's eyes. "He doesn't look it now — but he is a werewolf!" Dad declared.

"No, I'm not!" the man whined. "I told you a hundred times, you're making a big mistake!"

"Ignore him, Aaron."

44

I usually trust Dad's judgment. But it was hard to believe that this bald, shrimp of a guy could actually turn into a hairy beast.

"Are you sure, Dad?" I studied the man. The afternoon sun shone down on him. Small beads of sweat glistened on his shiny pink head. "He looks like an accountant, or a dentist, or maybe an eye doctor. He doesn't look like a flesh-eating beast."

"I'm not a werewolf. I swear." The little man moaned. "You have to believe me. I'm — I'm a vegetarian."

"He's a werewolf. I'm sure of it!" Dad pumped a fist in the air. "My dream has come true. I'm the only man in history to catch a real, live werewolf!"

Dad's eyes sparkled. I couldn't remember the last time I'd seen him so happy.

"We'll bring him home — and we'll get him on TV. We'll be the first to show the world a living werewolf!" Dad wrapped his arm around my shoulder. "We're going to be famous, Aaron. We're going to make a fortune with this creature! Now — let's get going!"

My father whistled as he lifted his backpack off the ground and slid it onto his back.

"You walk in front. I'll walk behind," Dad instructed. "The creature walks in the middle."

Dad turned to his prey. "Don't even think about giving us any trouble," he warned. "Let's go." He gave the little guy a shove.

The man stumbled forward. The chains around

his legs clanged as he shuffled into the forest. "You're making a big mistake!" he cried. "I told you — I'm a trapper. My name is Ben Grantley. I trap bears for their skins and furs."

"Yeah, right," Dad said. "You're a trapper. And I'm a ballerina!" Dad laughed at his joke.

"You can't do this to me," the man whined.

I glanced over my shoulder and stared at our prisoner. Can this little guy really be a werewolf? I wondered. Or is Dad making a horrible, horrible mistake?

What will happen to us if Dad is wrong?

That night, we boarded a ship that would take us home.

I know I should have been happy. This was the moment I'd been dreaming about since we got to Bratvia — going home.

But so many things didn't feel right.

Mr. Grantley was still chained up. Dad and I loaded him into a cage. But we needed help getting the cage onto the ship.

The deckhands took one look at the little man in the cage and thought Dad was nuts. But Dad insisted that Mr. Grantley was a killer. He flashed his sheriff's badge. And they finally agreed to help. They lowered the cage into the cargo hold for us.

That's where Mr. Grantley was going to stay during the long trip back. A whole week in the cargo hold — where it was really dark and really damp.

Dad and I were sharing a comfortable cabin.

I sank down into my big bed and closed my eyes.

I could still see the fear on Mr. Grantley's face as the cage was lowered into the bottom of the ship.

His cold had grown worse. His eyes were watery. His nose was red. He looked totally miserable — and so frightened.

I felt sorry for the poor guy.

I glanced over at Dad. He sat at a desk, tightly clutching the phone. He was talking to a lawyer back home. Making big plans for the werewolf's arrival.

Dad was so sure Mr. Grantley was a werewolf. But no matter how hard I tried, it was hard to believe.

As I listened to Dad on the phone, the ship pitched violently. Dad didn't seem to notice.

I felt dizzy. Seasick.

I concentrated on taking deep, regular breaths. I swallowed hard. I tried not to throw up.

"The sea is going to be rough and choppy," the ship's captain warned us earlier. "It will be like this the whole way home."

I don't think I can last a week on this ship, I thought as my stomach lurched.

"That's right!" Dad shouted into the phone. "Call the newspapers. The TV and radio stations.

Set up a website! Let everyone know what we're up to!"

Let everyone know what we're up to.

I couldn't believe what Dad was up to. He had plans and slogans for all kinds of new werewolf stuff:

Werewolf Running Shoes: To Run Ahead of the Pack!

Werewolf Raisin Squares: The Cereal with Bite!

Werewolf Sleepy-time Tea: To Tame the Wild Beast Inside You!

Werewolf Vitamins: For When You're Not Feeling Quite Human!

"A TV show?" Dad ran a hand through his thick brown hair. "Of course, we'll have a TV show! But it has to be live action. No cartoons! And don't forget the movie. We've got to make a movie deal!"

Dad stood up and nervously paced the small room. Listening. Nodding. Pacing faster. Talking louder into the phone.

The ship lurched to one side.

My stomach flip-flopped.

I felt dizzier.

My head ached.

"I don't know," Dad said into the phone. "Hold on." He turned to me. "Are you okay? You don't look right."

"I — I don't feel well," I moaned.

"It's seasickness," he said. "Go up on deck. Take a walk. Breathe in some fresh air. I'm sure that will help. I'll be up as soon as I get off the phone."

I staggered out of the cabin. It was belowdecks. I had a long hallway to walk down and a longer flight of steps to climb to get outside. I didn't think I was going to make it.

The ship reeled sharply from side to side.

I let out a loud groan as I struggled up the stairs.

I stumbled on deck.

It was chilly out here. But the cool, moist air felt good against my skin.

I took a deep breath. I could practically taste the sea salt.

My stomach felt a little less queasy. My head stopped spinning.

I stood against the railing and looked at the ocean.

So dark. I couldn't see where the water met the night sky.

I never stared into this kind of darkness before. No moon. No stars. I couldn't see a thing.

It's as if I'm trying to see with my eyes closed, I thought.

As I waited for Dad, a strong wind crashed against me.

The ship rocked violently.

I gripped the railing tightly as the wind pounded me with a force I didn't think possible.

"STORM!" I heard the distant cry of a deck-hand.

Another powerful gust battered the ship.

The ship pitched wildly.

A wave washed over the deck. Water poured over my shoes.

"HELP!" I shouted, clinging to the rail. "I NEED HELP!"

The wind muffled my cries.

I screamed again. But the wind roared so loudly, I couldn't hear *myself*!

Another high black wave crashed over the deck.

I gripped the rail.

Another wave rolled high in front of me.

And swept over me.

Cold. So cold and heavy.

I felt myself go under the darkness.

The rail disappeared.

And then the deck.

As the wave carried me . . . carried me into the churning black ocean.

I tried to scream.

I tried to swim.

But the powerful wave lifted me over the side.

I shut my eyes. Prepared to be swallowed up by the dark, tossing waves.

But something held me back.

Strong hands. Gripping my ankles.

Holding on to me. Holding me against the wave's brutal pull.

I felt myself dragged back, back.

Sputtering and coughing, I fell facedown on the deck.

I almost drowned! My whole body shook from the cold, from the horror of it.

I took deep breaths, struggling to steady myself. Then I rolled over — and gasped!

"Are you okay?" Ben Grantley asked. He hovered over me, his face filled with concern.

"H-how did you get out?" I stammered.

"The chains were loose. I needed some air. It was way too stuffy down there." He took off his glasses and tried to dry them on the sleeve of his drenched shirt. "Almost lost these in the wave. I can't see a thing without them," he said softly.

"You saved my life!" I sputtered.

"I was lucky," he replied. "I saw you start to go over the side. I grabbed your feet and pulled you back. That's all."

I couldn't believe this guy.

How could he be a werewolf? I thought.

I stared into his sad hazel eyes. He doesn't have the eyes of a wolf. He can't even see without eyeglasses. Dad is definitely wrong about him, I decided.

"Aaron, are you okay?" Dad ran up the steps to the deck two at a time. "What are *you* doing here?" Dad cried out when he saw Ben. He reached out and grabbed Ben roughly by the arm.

"It's okay, Dad," I told him. "You can let go of him. He saved my life!"

"I don't care! He's a dangerous creature!" Dad yelled. "I don't want you anywhere near him!"

"But Dad, he saved my life!" I protested. "Just look at him! Does he *look* dangerous?"

"He's a werewolf, Aaron," Dad insisted. "I'm warning you — don't be fooled."

"You're wrong," Ben insisted. He squirmed in Dad's grip. "Please — release me. Let me return home. We can all forget this ever happened."

Dad ignored him. He yanked Ben away from me. Then he called for help.

I watched Dad and two deckhands take our prisoner back to the cargo hold. "We'll need extra chains," I heard Dad say as I started down the steps to our cabin.

I changed into dry jeans and a gray sweatshirt. Then I sat up in bed and stared out my porthole.

I watched the rolling ocean waves. I felt them slam against the ship's side.

My stomach was beginning to feel queasy again.

I stared up into the night sky. The heavy clouds had parted. A half-moon hung over the rocking ship.

I started to feel dizzy.

My shoulder throbbed with pain.

I never told Dad that the werewolf bit me, I realized. I didn't want him to worry. But now it really hurt. Maybe I should have told him.

I slipped my hand inside my sweatshirt. I started to rub my shoulder — and gasped.

I leaped out of bed and charged into the bathroom.

I yanked my sweatshirt over my head.

I gazed into the mirror.

"What is *that*?" I cried in horror.

My shoulder was red and swollen — and covered with a disgusting patch of thick black fur.

rubbed my shoulder frantically, trying to brush the fur away.

It didn't work.

I grabbed the hairy tuft and tried to yank it out.

"Owww!" That didn't work, either.

What's going on? I wondered, staring at the ugly black patch.

I pulled my sweatshirt back on. I couldn't stand to look at my hairy shoulder.

I walked out of the bathroom just as Dad came into the cabin.

"Uh, Dad? I need to show you something."

"In a second." Dad peeled off his soaking-wet yellow slicker. He went into the bathroom and hung it over the tub.

"Dad —" I started again.

"One more minute, Aaron!" He sat down at the

desk and picked up the phone. "I need to make a quick call."

Twenty minutes later, Dad was still on the phone, talking to his lawyer again.

"Forget about MacWerewolf Burgers. It's not a good idea," I heard him say. "Oh — did you get in touch with those stuffed-animal people?" he asked. "Have they started the design for Wolfie yet?"

My shoulder began to burn and itch. I reached under my shirt and scratched it.

"Dad — I just need to talk to you for a second," I whispered.

"Soon. Soon." Dad waved me away.

I crawled into bed.

I pulled the covers up to my chin — and watched Dad talk on the phone. He was so excited. I hadn't seem him this happy in years.

Maybe I won't tell him about my shoulder, I decided. I'll keep it a secret. I don't want to spoil things for him.

Besides, it's just a little patch of hair — right?

No big deal.

Part Two

I — Aaron Freidus — live in a small town, in a very small house. Most of my friends live in big houses — with an "upstairs." We don't have an upstairs.

We have four small rooms — a kitchen, a living room, and two bedrooms. They're all on the same floor and steps away from each other.

Our kitchen is so small we have to keep the refrigerator in the living room. Our living room is so small we only have space for a small couch and my dad's desk — and the refrigerator.

But my house has something none of my friends' houses have. In the center of our very small living room we have a very large cage.

And inside the cage is a werewolf.

I — Aaron Freidus — have a werewolf in my living room.

Before we went to Bratvia to hunt down a were-wolf, only my friends thought that Dad was crazy.

But now the whole world knows about the werewolf in the living room.

And now the whole world thinks my dad is crazy.

What do I think?

Is Ben Grantley — the little bald guy sitting in a cage in the middle of my living room — really a werewolf?

I don't know. I just don't know. . . .

"Please, please, please, Aaron. Please let me come over to see the werewolf."

Every day after school, my best friend, Ashlee, begged to come over to see the werewolf. But Dad didn't want anyone to see him until tomorrow night.

Tomorrow night there will be a full moon.

"Tomorrow night," Dad told the world, "you will watch in wonder as an ordinary man changes into a snarling, hairy, half human, flesh-eating beast."

Dad wasn't the only one who didn't want *anyone* to see Ben.

Neither did I.

But Ashlee wouldn't give up.

"I'll do your homework for a week. No, a year. No, *ten* years!"

"Forget it, Ashlee."

"I'll clean your room for a year. No, your whole

house. No, your whole house and your dog's house too."

"I don't have a dog."

"If you had one, I'd clean his house. Please let me see the werewolf. Please, please, please. I want to be the first one to see him. *Please!*"

"Give it up, Ashlee."

"If you don't let me see him, I'll never talk to you again. I mean it. I'm not kidding. I'm serious."

"Ashlee — shut up!"

"I'll shut up if you let me see him. I'll be quiet. I won't say a word."

Yeah, right, I thought.

Ashlee never shuts up. She talks way too much. In fact, almost *everything* about Ashlee is too much!

She has wild blond hair that hangs down to her waist. Very bushy, very curly. But she puffs it up to make it look even bigger.

She's really tall — at least a foot taller than I am — but she wears platform sneakers to look even taller.

Her clothes are too much too. She likes to wear the layered look. For Ashlee, that means lots and lots of layers.

Today she had on a short-sleeved red T-shirt. Over that, a long-sleeved bright-yellow V-neck sweater. Over that, a low, scoop-neck orange sweatshirt with the sleeves cut off. She always makes sure all the colors show.

The red Lycra leggings she wore were covered with orange boxer shorts. If she could wear two pairs of shoes at the same time, she would. But she can't. So she wears one purple sneaker and one black one.

Every one of her fingers has a silver ring on it. And she wears three earrings in each ear.

I told you she's too much.

But she's my best friend — so what choice did I have? I had to let her see the werewolf.

"When can I see him?" Ashley begged on our way home from school. "I'll do anything for you. Just name it. Whatever. I'll do it. Can I see him?"

"Come home with me, and you can see him. Okay?"

"No," she said.

"What?"

"I have to go home first — to walk Madame Colette. Then I'll come over."

Madame Colette is Ashlee's miniature French poodle. Ashlee loves her. She insists that Madame Colette is so perfect, she's going to win the local dog show.

To tell you the truth, I think the dog looks like a fuzzy rat.

After Ashlee walked the dog, she came over to my house.

"That's *him*?" She pushed past me and headed straight for the living room. Her big blue eyes

64

grew wide as she circled the cage. She studied Ben Grantley from every angle.

Mr. Grantley sat cross-legged on the cage floor, with his head hanging down, his shoulders hunched.

He glanced up, gave Ashlee a weak smile, then lowered his head again.

"But Aaron — he's just a man. A normal-looking person. How can you keep him a prisoner like that? It's horrible. Disgusting. Awful. It's —"

"Dad captured him," I said bluntly. "He's a werewolf."

Ashlee kept insisting that Ben wasn't a were-wolf. I had to keep insisting that he was.

What could I say?

I didn't really think Ben was a werewolf. But I didn't want Ashlee to think I was the kind of kid who let his father keep a normal human being locked up in a cage in the middle of the living room.

"I don't know about this, Aaron. . . ." She walked right up to the cage bars.

Before I knew what she was doing —

Before I could stop her —

Ashlee pushed her hand through the bars.

Ben leaped to his feet.

"NO! Ashlee! Don't get close!" I screamed. "Stay back!"

"*C*hill out, Aaron!* I'm just giving him a candy bar. Look at him. He's starving. When was the last time you fed this guy?"

"Dad *must* have given him breakfast this morning. I think," I murmured.

"Thank you," Ben said softly. He took the candy bar from Ashlee and unwrapped it. "My name is Ben. I'm not a werewolf," he told her. "They've made a terrible mistake."

Ashlee narrowed her big blue eyes at me. "Your dad is crazy. Insane!" she screamed.

"Calm down!" I yelled back.

"I'm not kidding," Ashley insisted. "Your father has totally lost his mind."

66

She didn't say another word. She turned — and stormed out of the house.

I gazed at Ben. He sat huddled in the corner of his cage. He took a small bite out of the candy bar. Then he stared off into space.

He looked miserable.

I felt miserable looking at him.

A few minutes later, I heard a knock on our door. It was the satellite crew. They had come to set up the satellite hookup so the whole world could watch Ben transform into a werewolf tomorrow night.

The satellite guys ran wires from the living room to our rooftop. I heard two of them laughing. "This guy can't be a werewolf," one of them snickered.

"The sheriff has totally lost it," his partner replied, shaking his head.

Ben watched them. He paced his cage nervously. Beads of sweat puddled on his bald, pink head.

What have we done to this poor guy? I thought. This just isn't right. Ashlee and the satellite guys are right. Dad has made a horrible mistake.

But what can I do? What can I do?

The next day after school, I didn't want to go home.

I didn't want to look at Ben. I didn't want to

stare into his sad eyes. I didn't want to watch him pace his cage.

But I had to go home. I promised Dad I'd help make sure everything was set for the broadcast.

I won't go into the living room, I decided as I stepped into the house. I'll head straight for my bedroom.

I closed the front door quietly.

I started to my room.

"Aaron — is that you?" Ben called softly.

I let out a sigh.

"Yeah, it's me." I went in to see him.

"Aaron, please listen." Ben stood up and pressed his pudgy face against the cage bars.

"I'm not a werewolf. Your father should have checked with the Forest Patrol. They would have told him the truth. My name really is Ben Grantley, and I'm a licensed fur trapper."

"I'm sorry." I shook my head. "There's nothing I can do."

I set my backpack down on the floor. I leaned over and rummaged through it. "Here. I brought you a candy bar."

"Where did you get that?" Ben asked as I straightened up.

"From the grocery store."

"No. That." Ben pointed to the werewolf tooth that had swung free of my shirt. "The sign of the werewolf!"

"I guess *you* must have given it to me. When you were a wolf."

Ben stared at the tooth. "No. I didn't, Aaron. I've never actually seen one before. Only heard about them. The werewolf gave it to you. Not me. I'm only a trapper."

"What else do you know about it?" I asked.

"That's it." Ben shrugged.

I slipped my hand through the cage and handed him the candy.

"You have to help me!" He let the candy drop to the floor.

"I'm sorry," I apologized again. "I wish I could. But it's too late."

"It's not too late," he insisted. "Do you want your dad to embarrass himself? He's going to ruin his whole life in front of the entire world — unless you help him."

"But what can I do?"

"Let me go. I promise, Aaron, you'll be glad you did. Please — let me go. Do your dad a big favor. Unlock the cage. Let me go."

I stared through the bars at him — at the hopelessness in his eyes.

Should I let him go? I wondered. Should I?

My mind raced.

He saved my life on the ship, I remembered. I owed him a favor.

He isn't a werewolf. He can't be a werewolf.

I don't want Dad to be embarrassed in front of the world.

I reached into the top drawer of our desk.

I found the key to the cage.

I slipped the key into the lock and opened the door.

18

"Thank you! Thank you!" Ben sprang out of the cage.

"You won't regret this, Aaron!" he cried. "You've done the right thing. You'll see."

He gave me a big hug, then ran out of the house.

An hour later, I heard Dad's car pull up the driveway.

I ran to the front door to meet him.

"Ready for the big night?" Dad asked with a broad smile.

"Um. Dad. I have to tell you something."

"Sure. Let's go in the living room," he said.

"Wait." I grabbed his arm. "Don't go in there yet."

"What's wrong?" Dad locked his eyes on mine.

"I — I let Ben out," I confessed.

"You *what*?" Dad spun around and charged into

the living room. He stared at the empty cage in disbelief. "How could you do this?" he cried. He began pacing the room.

"I — I felt sorry for him," I murmured. "And I — I didn't want you to make a terrible mistake. Everyone was *laughing* at you, Dad!"

"Do you know what you did?" Dad stopped pacing in front of me. *"You let out a werewolf!"* He screamed so loud the veins in his neck popped out. "Do you know what he's going to do tonight, Aaron? He's going to turn into a wolf and kill innocent people — all because of you!"

"But Dad —"

"I don't want to hear another word from you," he yelled. "I don't even want to look at you. Go to your room!"

I went to my room and threw myself on my bed. I did the right thing, I told myself.

But will Dad ever forgive me?

"That's right!" I could hear Dad yelling into the phone. "The werewolf has escaped. Send out all our officers. They have to search the area. We have to find the creature before sunset."

Dad was talking to his police officers on our speakerphone. I could hear some of the officers laughing in the background.

"Are you sure you want us to do this?" an officer asked. "Haven't you taken this werewolf thing a bit too far, Sheriff?"

"Don't question me!" Dad barked into the

phone. "Just do it!" I could hear him stomping around the living room. Slamming doors. Screaming into the phone some more.

I know I did the right thing. Ben is *not* a werewolf, I told myself again and again.

So why did I suddenly feel sick?

My head began to ache. I felt light-headed. I closed my eyes.

"Call the fire department!" Dad ordered. "Get those guys searching too. We're going to need all the help we can get!"

I fell asleep to the sound of Dad shouting into the phone. When I woke up, it was dark out.

I sat up in bed — and the room began to spin around me.

What's wrong with me? I wondered. Maybe I just need something to eat. I missed dinner.

I climbed out of bed. Walked past my mirror — and screamed.

Thick black fur sprouted from my face, my arms, my legs. From my wolf snout. From my huge paws.

I curled back my lips — and gasped. I had glistening fangs!

"I'm a werewolf!" I groaned.

Before I could stop myself, I charged for the bedroom window — and leaped out. I landed on all fours.

Running now.

Running through my backyard.

Running down our street.

Running ... running ... the air felt so cool on my hot fur.

It felt so good to run.

Running through the darkness ... I felt as if I could run forever.

19

I opened my eyes. Then closed them quickly to shut out the bright morning sunlight.

Where am I?

I glanced around groggily.

Why am I on my bedroom floor? Did I fall out of bed?

I stood up. Stretched. Let out a long yawn.

I felt so tired. As if I hadn't slept.

I desperately wanted to go back to sleep. But I knew Dad would be angry with me if I did. So, yawning and stretching, I headed into the kitchen for breakfast.

I poured a glass of orange juice and a bowl of raisin squares cereal. Then I sat down to eat. The TV in the kitchen was on.

"Two women and a man were attacked as they left here last night." The news reporter pointed to the movie theater behind him. "The two women are recovering in the hospital from the vicious, brutal attack."

Vicious, brutal attack?

In our small town?

What's going on? I wondered. I gazed at the TV.

"This woman saw the whole thing." The reporter turned to a blond woman in her twenties.

"It was a wild wolf-creature!" the woman's voice trembled. "I've never seen anything like it before. It was terrifying."

"A wild wolf-creature? Oh, noooo!" I moaned.

I leaned over the table to get closer to the TV. "What happened to the third victim? Tell us!" I yelled at the screen. "Please," I prayed. "Don't say he's dead."

"The third victim —"

I held my breath.

"— escaped with a few scratches."

I let out a long sigh of relief.

"Reports have also come in from across town," the reporter continued. "From the Village Arena Dog Show, where the creature burst into the show — and viciously attacked several dogs."

"What have I done?" I cried. "This is all my fault! Ben lied to me! I let the werewolf loose!"

I snapped off the TV. I didn't want to hear any more.

"Ben really is a werewolf," I groaned. "Dad was right! I should never have doubted him."

My stomach heaved. My whole body shook.

Now what? I wondered.

Dad will never, never forgive me.

The whole world will never, never forgive me.

I trudged into my room and closed the door. I wanted to hide in there forever.

I glanced down at the floor — where yesterday's clothes were scattered. Disgusted with myself, I kicked the clothes across the floor. They slid under the bed.

"Smart move, Aaron." I shook my head. "Now you'll have to crawl under there and get them."

I got down on my stomach. I crawled under the bed and pulled out the clothes.

I picked them up — and cried out.

My jeans and T-shirt were ripped to shreds — and covered in blood!

20

"What have I done?" I gaped at my bloody clothes.

I closed my eyes — and tried to recall where I was last night. What I did.

I remembered not feeling well. Then falling asleep.

"Oh, nooo," I groaned as I remembered staring into my mirror. Remembered the hairy beast that stared back at me. Remembered jumping out my bedroom window.

My eyes darted to the window.

Yes — it stood wide open.

Now I remembered everything. My furry body. Running on all fours.

"I'm the werewolf!" My legs began to tremble. "*I'm* the one who attacked those people and the dogs last night!"

I sat down on my bed and thought back to that strange night in the forest. When the werewolf bit me.

He turned *me* into a werewolf, I realized. I shook my head, stunned.

"That's why the creature passed the tooth to me. It's the sign of the werewolf. That's *me* now. I'm a werewolf."

My stomach twisted into a painful knot.

Ben told the truth, I realized. *I* did those horrible things last night — not Ben.

I stood up and gazed into the mirror.

No sign of fur.

No paws.

I spread my lips wide. "No fangs." I sighed with relief. But that moon.

"*Tonight* is another full moon!" I gasped.

Someone has to help me!

Someone has to keep me inside. I can't go out. I don't want to hurt anyone else!

"DAD! DAD!" I rushed out of my bedroom to find my father. "Dad — listen to me!" I burst into the living room. "I'm the werewolf! Not Ben! It's me!"

The living room was empty.

"Dad? Are you here?"

No answer. But I saw a yellow piece of paper on the desk. A note from Dad:

Aaron,

The werewolf attacked last night. Had to go down to the station house to meet with my officers. Don't know when I'll be back. Come home right after school. And don't go out tonight!

Love,
Dad

"Now what am I going to do?" I groaned.

I'll lock myself in my bedroom, I decided. I'll make sure there's no way I can get out. That way, I won't be able to hurt anyone.

I decided not to go to school. I had too much to do to get ready for tonight.

I got dressed quickly and ran to the lumberyard. I bought boxes and boxes of nails, wooden planks, and heavy-duty rope.

I told the owner that the stuff was for my father, so he agreed to deliver it to our house by lunchtime.

It took me all afternoon to nail my bedroom windows shut. As I pounded in the last nail, the phone rang. It was Ashlee.

"I can't believe it!" she exclaimed. "That little guy in the cage — he really is a werewolf. Your father isn't nuts."

I couldn't tell Ashlee the truth. I couldn't tell her that I was the werewolf.

"How did that monster escape?" she went on.

"I let him out."

"You *what*?" she shrieked. "Are you *crazy*?"

"What are you talking about? You were the one who said he was definitely *not* a werewolf! You *wanted* me to set him free!" I shouted back.

"That was before the dog show!" she wailed. "Before he ate Madame Colette!"

"Oooooh," I moaned softly.

I ate Madame Colette last night. I ate my best friend's dog!

"I — I have to go, Ashlee. I feel sick." I hung up the phone and started to gag.

Struggling to keep my breakfast down, I staggered to my room. Tested out the windows. Made sure they were nailed tight.

Then I hammered the wooden planks across my door. Finally, I wound heavy-duty rope around my waist and tied myself to the dresser.

That should do it, I decided. This will definitely keep me from attacking again tonight.

I hope.

22

I sat on my bed — stared out the window — and waited.

I watched the sun slowly set.

As dusk turned to night, I saw the full moon rise in the sky — and felt my skin begin to tingle. Then burn.

I gazed in the mirror — and saw dark fur sprout over my skin.

My back and chest began to throb. I could see the muscles pulsating, straining against my T-shirt. Then a searing pain shot though my body as my bulging muscles tore through my clothes.

I squeezed my eyes shut as the bones in my face shifted. Formed into a skull that was half human, half beast.

I let out a howl of agony as fangs exploded from my gums.

Then a fiery pain shot through my hands and feet. I gazed at them in horror as my fingers and toes shrank. As my hands and feet formed into paws. As razor-sharp claws sprang from my scalding skin.

I burned with fever.

Burned with hunger.

With an ugly roar, I grabbed the rope around my waist and tore it away.

With the fury of a wild animal, I ripped the planks from my bedroom door.

And then I was running.

Running out of the house.

Running on all fours through the cool night air.

Running — with a raging, bloodthirsty hunger — in search of fresh meat!

My sharp wolf eyes spotted them — a boy and a girl. Standing on the corner in the shadow of an oak tree. Talking. Unaware.

I knew them. They were sixth graders in my school.

An overwhelming hunger washed over me.

I could smell the scent of their skin. I could practically taste their soft, warm flesh. I ran my tongue over my dripping fangs.

They started walking.

I ran in the shadows, stalking them.

"Did you hear something?" The boy stopped abruptly. He turned and looked in my direction.

I dove behind a tall hedge, out of sight.

The two continued walking. Glancing back every few steps. Walking faster.

I could smell the sweat on their skin.

I could smell their fear.

I was repulsed by my hunger. Repulsed and driven by it at the same time. I had no control. I had to eat. I had to eat — now!

They stopped again.

Glanced back.

"I think we're being followed," the boy said tensely.

"I know," the girl agreed. "I have the same feeling. It's so creepy." She shivered.

"Come on. I don't like this." The boy grabbed the girl's hand.

They started to run.

I sprang from the shadows. Let out a deep growl. Leaped at them.

They spun around to look at me.

Their eyes grew wide with terror.

The girl screamed.

"The werewolf!" the boy gasped. He clutched the girl's arm tightly, and they took off.

I sprinted after them.

"There it is! The werewolf! *Get it!*" I heard shouts behind me.

I turned and saw a police patrol car. Two officers. Heads out the window. Pointing and shouting.

Another head shot out of the back window. It was my father!

"Call for backup!" he commanded. Then he leaped out of the car and started to chase me.

"Creature has been spotted. Officers in pursuit!" an excited voice squawked over the patrol car radio.

I ran faster.

The car doors flew open. The two officers jumped out and joined the chase.

"He's getting away!"

"Head him off!"

Their cries of panic rang in my ears.

I ran on all fours. Panting deeply. Heart pounding. Running faster than I thought I could.

I reached a corner. Bolted across the street. Heard the wail of sirens. Turned toward the sound. Saw the flash of angry red lights.

"Run faster. Faster," I told myself.

I heard the pounding of feet behind me. Gaining on me.

I fled into the school yard.

"We've got him now!" I heard my father's excited cry. And then the clang of a metal gate as it crashed closed.

I stood in the middle of the yard. I turned — and saw a line of cops standing just inside the gate.

A fleet of patrol cars skidded to a stop. Their headlights lit up the yard with a harsh glare.

I squinted into the bright light.

My father stepped forward.

He slowly made his way toward me.

"You're surrounded. You can't escape," he said. "It's over."

24

"That's it. Stay right there." Dad continued to walk toward me. The other officers remained at the gate, watching in silence.

I stood in the glare of the headlights, staring at Dad, frozen.

Then I heard breathing. From behind me.

I whirled around — too late.

As my dad walked toward me, several officers approached from behind.

"Got him!" one of them screamed as he dove for me. He grabbed me around the middle. Wrestled me to the ground.

I let out a shattering howl.

I snapped my head around — and tried to dig my teeth into the officer's arm.

I missed.

But the startled officer released his grip.

Now all the officers stormed at me — from in front and behind — with their clubs raised high.

I glanced frantically left and right.

No way out.

No way to escape — unless I leaped over the metal fence.

With a furious growl, I charged the fence. Leaned back on my haunches. Leaped high.

The fence rattled from my weight as I clambered up.

I reached the top — and the fence began to shake violently.

I swayed with it. Nearly fell off.

I glanced down.

Police officers held the fence and rocked it, trying to shake me loose.

I leaped over the fence — onto the school roof — and saw another group of officers charging at me.

Oh, no! Dad had men up here too!

"Don't let him get away!" I heard Dad shout from down below.

I raced across the rooftop — reached the end — and jumped to the next roof and the next.

I'm safe up here. They can't get me now, I thought. I slowed down — and heard the roar of a helicopter overhead.

I gazed up — and saw the police chopper aiming straight for me. Its bright search beam swept the rooftops. Searching for me.

I let out a long howl. Then leaped down to the ground. I ran on all fours in the shadows.

Sirens wailed through the neighborhood. I heard the screech of tires as fire engines turned sharp corners, hunting me down.

I raced through backyards.

House lights flashed on. Sirens wailed. Frightened shouts wailed in my ears.

I ran harder — but my lungs burned.

Stop, I told myself.

Rest.

Find someplace to hide.

In a backyard up ahead, I spotted a small shed. I glanced at the house. It was dark.

I crept up to the shed.

A latch on the door swung free. No lock on it.

I pushed the door open, slipped inside, and shoved the door closed again. I wedged myself between a lawn mower and a bicycle and collapsed onto the wooden floor.

My legs trembled with pain.

My chest heaved as I tried to catch my breath.

But my pounding heart was beginning to slow.

"Everything will be okay," I told myself. "You're safe here. The sun should be rising soon. You'll turn back to normal — and sneak home."

As I let my eyes slowly close — the shed door opened with a *BANG*!

A bright, blinding light flooded the shed.

"We've *got him*!" an officer shouted. "We've got him *trapped*!"

I leaped up.

My eyes darted around the shed.

No windows.

No way to escape.

I returned my gaze to the door. I threw back my head and let out a long, loud howl.

The police raised their guns.

An officer raised his pistol. Aimed it at me. "I've got him," he told the others. "This guy is history."

He tightened his finger on the trigger.

25

on't shoot!* That's my son!" I heard Dad cry out.

Huh?

How does he know? How does he know it's me?

Dad crashed through the startled officers. "Are you okay?" he cried. He glanced outside — peered up at the night sky. "It's almost dawn. You'll be safe here until then."

He ordered his officers to stand back. Then he strode out of the shed and closed the door.

I could hear the officers outside arguing with him.

"He's a killer!" one of them yelled.

"He has to be destroyed!"

I glanced down at my body. I was still a beast. I wasn't changing back.

What if something goes wrong?

What if I don't change back this time?

I peered through a slit in the shed's wooden planks. It was still dark out.

My heart pounded as I waited for the sun to rise.

"Sheriff Freidus — you've lost your judgment!" another angry voice called out. "That creature can't be your son!"

A fist slammed against the shed door. The door opened with a *BANG*! "He has to be killed!"

Shaking, I dodged behind a crate.

"I told you to stand back!" Dad ordered. A hand reached in and closed the shed door again.

I let out a sigh — and felt my skin begin to tingle.

"Get him! Get him!" A furious chant rose up from the police officers.

As the angry voices rose, my wolf skin began to shed.

"Kill the beast! Get him!" the men's voices grew louder, angrier.

Hurry! Hurry! I stared down at my body. Change faster! Before it's too late!

My legs burned.

My head ached.

My skin felt as if it was being torn from my bones.

I howled in agony. Howled until my throat ached.

"Listen to him. He's *not* your son. He's a beast! Listen to him howl!"

"Shoot him!"

The door slammed open. An officer stood in front of me — with his gun drawn.

"Dad?" I called out weakly.

My father shoved the man aside. "Aaron!" Dad rushed over. He sat down on the floor with me. Threw his arms around my shoulders and gave me a tight hug. "Don't worry. Everything will be okay!"

I stared down at my body. My normal body!

"It *is* his son! It's really Aaron." I heard hushed whispers outside.

"How did you know, Dad?" I asked, my voice still weak. "How did you know it was me?"

"The tooth." Dad pointed to the werewolf tooth hanging around my neck. "I saw the tooth — and I knew it was you. But I didn't see it until you ran toward the shed. I wish I had seen it sooner. Sorry, Aaron."

I clutched the tooth.

It saved my life again, I realized.

"Let's go home." Dad helped me to my feet.

I stepped out of the shed. The morning light stung my eyes. I shut them quickly. When I opened them, I saw a mob of police officers staring at me.

"We'll take him now, sir." A police officer grabbed my arm tightly.

"Leave him alone." My dad brushed the officer away.

"That's not possible, sir." The officer grabbed my arm again.

The other officers nodded in agreement.

They moved forward slowly, forming a tight circle around us.

"Dad?" My voice shook. "What are they going to do to me?"

"**L**eave . . . him . . . alone!" Dad's face turned red with fury. The mob of officers backed off.

"I want to take Aaron home." Dad spoke calmly now. "He doesn't want to hurt anyone. He needs help."

"What will happen during the next full moon? What if he attacks again?" an officer asked.

"He won't," Dad promised. "I'll take responsibility for him. I'll make sure he never harms anyone. I ask only one favor. Please, don't tell anyone about Aaron's problem. He'll never have a normal life if the whole town knows about him."

The officers stepped back and let us go.

One of the men drove Dad and me home in a squad car. Exhausted from the chase, I slumped back in the seat and rode in silence.

When we arrived home, I felt much better. "I should have told you about this sooner," I said as we headed into the living room.

"When did it happen? *How* did it happen?" Dad ran a hand through his blond hair. His blue eyes filled with sadness. He sat down on the couch and loosened his shirt collar. His broad shoulders sagged as he leaned back and waited for my answer.

"It happened the night the werewolf jumped me in the forest," I explained. "He bit my shoulder. I know I should have told you then. But I didn't want to spoil things for you. You were so happy."

"I'm sorry, Aaron." Dad shook his head. "I was too obsessed with finding a werewolf. I should have taken better care of you. I should never have let any of this happen."

Dad buried his head in his hands. "Thank you, Aaron," he murmured.

"Thank you? For what, Dad?"

"For letting Ben go." He glanced up at me. "He wasn't the werewolf. You were right. I would have embarrassed myself in front of the whole world if it weren't for you. I feel like a total fool."

Dad stood up.

He began pacing the room.

"Don't worry. Everything is going to change." His voice grew stronger. "I'm going to devote myself to you now, Aaron. I'm going to quit the police force. I'm going to spend the rest of my life finding a cure for you! And I don't care how long it takes —"

The phone rang.

Dad picked it up.

He listened to the voice on the other end. His eyes narrowed. The muscles in his face tightened. "That can't be possible!" he shouted into the phone.

He listened some more, then hung up the phone.

"What is it, Dad? What's wrong?"

"That was the police station." Dad took a deep breath. "A werewolf has attacked six people across town."

"It wasn't me!" I leaped up from the couch. "You know that — right?"

"I know," Dad said. "It couldn't have been you. The attack was way across town. And it happened at the same time you were in the school yard."

"Then who did it, Dad?" I shook my head, confused.

"It had to be Ben." Dad planted his hands on his hips. "He lied to us! He *is* a werewolf!"

Ben really is a werewolf, I thought with disbelief. And he's out there — somewhere.

"When is the next full moon, Dad?" I asked in a trembling voice.

"It's tonight." Dad sighed. "Only one more night of the full moon," he said, closing his eyes, thinking.

"What are you going to do?" I asked.

"I have a plan." Dad's eyes flew open. "I'll lead the search for Ben tonight. I'll arm the men with automatic rifles. I'm sorry, Aaron," Dad said softly. "But we're going to have to shoot to kill."

As the sun set, I watched Dad get ready. He removed his rifle from the glass case that hung on the living room wall.

He filled each chamber with a silver bullet.

"Do you really think it takes a silver bullet to kill a werewolf?" I shuddered.

"That's what the legends say. I don't know if it's true or not," he answered. "But why take chances?"

Poor Ben.

I knew he was a werewolf. A killer. But I couldn't help feeling sorry for him. And sorry for myself.

"Okay. It's time." Dad nodded toward the cage in the living room.

Dad made me climb into the cage.

"You'll be safe in there," he said, chaining the door, then locking it with a huge metal padlock.

I stared out through the living room window and watched the moon rise.

I thought about Ben.

How he saved my life on the ship.

I wrapped my hand around the werewolf tooth. Ben was the one who gave it to me.

That means he saved my life twice! I realized.

I have to try to help him, I thought. I have to warn him.

I grabbed the cage bars and shook them. "How can I help him if I'm locked in here?" I wailed.

The doorbell rang.

"Come in!" I shouted. "Hurry!"

"What are you doing in there?" Ashlee peered into the living room. "Aaron — is this some kind of a joke?"

"No joke," I murmured. I had an idea.

"The werewolf tricked me," I told Ashlee. "He came back here. He locked me in the cage — and escaped again. Quick — let me out. I have to warn my dad!"

"Okay." Ashlee glanced around the living room. "Where's the key?"

Good question.

I didn't watch Dad after he locked me in. I didn't know where he put the key.

"Try the desk drawers!"

Ashlee rummaged through the drawers. "Not here," she reported.

"We have to find the key!" I cried.

"Calm down, Aaron," she said. "I have a better idea. In fact, it's a really great idea. It's brilliant. It's —"

"Ashlee — we don't have time!"

"All right. All right. We don't need the key." She smiled.

"We don't?"

"Nope. *I'll* find your father and warn him about Ben. When your father comes home, he can saw you out or something."

"Not a good idea, Ashlee."

"Why not?"

Why not? Why not?

What could I tell her?

"Because —" I glanced out the window. "I don't want you to go out there now. The full moon is rising. It's too dangerous."

"You're right." Ashlee didn't hesitate. "I'll find the key."

As Ashlee searched the house, I began to feel my skin tingle.

I can't let Ashlee see me change! I told myself. What am I going to do?

"Hurry, Ashlee! Hurry!" I shouted, unable to hide my panic.

My skin began to burn.

My head began to ache.

Where did Dad put the key? What if he took it with him? I groaned.

And then I thought of the cookie jar!

That's where Dad stores the extra set of house keys!

"Check the cookie jar on the kitchen counter!" I called.

"Got it!" Ashlee sang out. She skipped into the living room, waving the key in the air.

"Hurry up!"

"Okay. Okay." She slipped the key into the lock and opened the door.

"You'd better hurry home." I sprang out of the cage.

I could feel the fur begin to sprout on my back.

"Are you crazy? I'm not going out there. It's too dangerous. You said so yourself!"

"You — you can't wait here!" I stammered. "The werewolf — he might come back here. You have to go home. It's safer there. Run!"

"I guess." Ashlee headed for the front door.

My muscles began to pound.

Ashlee grabbed the doorknob.

I glanced down — and saw dark, bristly hair begin to sprout from my hands.

Don't turn back, Ashlee, I silently begged.

Please — go out the door. Don't turn around.

Please — don't see what I've become.

28

Ashlee turned the doorknob. "Good luck, Aaron," she called back to me.

I didn't speak. I stood still, paralyzed with fear.

She opened the door.

She looked left, then right. "I guess it's safe to go out," she murmured.

I didn't reply.

She stood in the doorway, gazing out. She glanced up at the moon.

A sharp pain shot through my skull as my head turned half human, half creature.

"Oh, well," Ashlee took a deep breath. "I'm going, Aaron. Call me later."

Leave! Don't turn around. Just leave, I prayed again.

"Be careful," she said. She closed the door behind her and left.

I ran to the window. Watched her run down the moonlit street. Then I raced through the house and charged out the back door.

A searing pain shot through my mouth as my fangs slipped out. I howled in agony.

The transformation was complete.

I was a total wolf-creature now.

I huddled in the shadow of our house. Thinking.

Where should I go?

Where is Ben?

Will I find him in time to save him? My heart began to pound.

"The werewolf!" a woman's voice screamed.

I froze.

"Help me! HELP! He's attacking me!"

My eyes darted down the row of backyards — and I saw the werewolf. A few houses away.

He curled back his lips and snarled at the woman. He skulked forward. Pinned the woman against her house, trapping her there.

I let out an angry roar — and charged.

I leaped over high fences. Tore through the backyards. Then leaned back on my haunches. Took a deep breath — and dove at the werewolf.

With a sharp howl, the startled creature backed away.

The woman's eyes bulged at me. She shrieked in terror. Spun off the wall — and ran.

I stood face-to-face with the werewolf. His fur bristled as he began to circle me.

He curled back his lips — and bared his fangs.

What is he going to do? I wondered. Is he going to attack *me*?

I trained my eyes on him. And let out a low, menacing snarl.

Is this how it's going to end? I wondered. Will the two of us battle each other — until one of us is dead?

29

"This way! Down this street!" an officer shouted. "I hear something!"

"Circle around back!" I heard my father command. "Don't let the creature escape!"

The police are here. They're closing in! I realized.

I stared at the werewolf. His ears pricked up. His dark, glowing eyes darted left and right. Searching for a place to hide.

How can I help him?

How can I save his life?

If only the creature could change back to being Ben. No one would shoot a little bald guy!

I pictured Dad loading his rifle with the silver bullets. Would a silver bullet kill the werewolf? I didn't want to find out.

Wait a second.

I read some werewolf legends too. There was a way to make a werewolf change back to human form, I remembered. But what was it?

"Think! Think!" I told myself.

Yes! I remembered.

To get a werewolf to change back to human form, you had to say the creature's real name.

I could do that!

I knew his real name!

Would it work? I had to try.

I turned to the creature. I stared directly into his gleaming black eyes.

"Ben!" I shouted. "Ben Grantley!"

But my shouts came out as wolf grunts.

Nothing happened.

"Work in pairs!" I heard my father order his men. "Search every yard!"

There was another way to get a werewolf to turn human again. What was it?

The wail of sirens rose through the night air.

I couldn't think straight.

"Concentrate, Aaron!" My head pounded as I tried to remember.

Got it!

I had to knock on the werewolf's head three times!

"How can I *do* that?" I howled. "He won't stand still for that!"

"I heard the creature!" an officer shouted. "We're getting closer!"

No more time.

I leaped at the creature.

Before he knew what was happening, I was on top of him. I swung my paw. Hit him in the head.

Once.

Twice.

Three times.

I leaped away.

No.

Nothing happened.

The creature let out a piercing howl. He glared at me with his terrifying eyes.

"This way, Sheriff Freidus!" a voice called. "In the next yard."

Heavy boots pounded the driveway.

I glanced frantically around the yard — and saw that my tooth pendant had slipped from my neck.

I grabbed it off the ground. And with a frantic motion, swung it around the werewolf's neck.

The officer burst into the yard.

I dodged behind a bush.

Hundreds of police stormed in.

The werewolf stared at them, frozen. Panting in fright. Cornered.

The police raised their rifles.

"I'm going to shoot!" an officer screamed.

I watched in horror as he took aim.

I heard the sharp click of his finger on the trigger — then the terrifying explosion as he opened fire.

30

The rifle flew up in the air — as Dad shoved the barrel up and away. The bullets flew harmlessly to the sky.

"Don't shoot!" Dad cried. "That's my son!"

Yes! I cheered from behind the bush. The tooth switch had worked. Dad thought the creature was me. I saved Ben's life!

The officers pounced on the werewolf. Flattened him to the ground. The werewolf snarled. Snapped his jaws. Writhed under the attack.

I watched from the shadows. Please don't hurt him, I thought.

The creature's legs flailed. He wrestled furiously to free himself. But there were too many men to fight off.

As his legs were bound with a heavy rope, a low, sad moan escaped the creature's throat.

His eyes clouded over. He knew he had lost. In one last act of defiance, he opened his mouth wide and angrily snapped his jaws.

A steel muzzle was quickly slipped over the creature's snout.

"Be careful. Don't hurt him." Dad's voice trembled as he stared at the defeated beast. "I don't know how my boy escaped. It won't happen again. I promise."

Dad and two of his officers drove the werewolf to my home.

I waited until all the officers left. Then, hiding in the shadows, I returned home too.

I stole through the back door. Peered into the living room. "It's not your fault, Aaron." Dad gently led the werewolf to the cage.

He untied the ropes. Removed the muzzle.

The creature snapped at Dad. But Dad leaped away quickly, unharmed.

"I'll have to find a stronger cage for you." Dad swung the cage door shut. "Don't worry. I'll take care of everything," he said, snapping the lock.

The werewolf threw back his head and howled.

I leaped into the living room.

"Ben — you're back!" Dad stared at me and gasped. "TWO werewolves. I have *two* werewolves in my living room! What do I do now?"

Dad jumped away from me.

I stretched out on the floor. Let out a soft

whimper, trying to let him know I wouldn't harm him.

"Good," Dad said softly. "Stay."

He sat down on the couch. Glanced at me, then at the werewolf in the cage, then back to me.

"I'm so sorry." He shook his head. "I have no choice. I must surrender you both to my officers."

My head jerked up. What was Dad saying? He didn't really mean that — did he?

"Too many lives are at stake. I can't take responsibility for both of you. I can't take responsibility for what the two of you might do."

No! He can't do this to us! I thought.

"I'm so sorry," he repeated. "All my life I dreamed of catching a werewolf. It was all I could think about. But it was a stupid, stupid dream. Now I've ruined all our lives. I'm heartbroken." Dad lowered his head sadly.

He'll change his mind. He won't turn us in, I thought. I'm his son. He wouldn't do that to his own son!

Dad jumped up from the couch. "I know what I'll do." He started pacing the room. "Everything is going to be okay!" he declared. "I'm going to talk to the top scientists in the country."

Yes! I knew it! I knew Dad would come up with a better idea. I knew he wouldn't turn on his own son!

"I know I ruined our lives. But I'll fix that. I

promise. Even if you both are locked away in a prison — I will work with the scientists. I will devote my life to finding a cure for both of you!"

Dad snatched up the phone. He punched in the police station number. "I have two werewolves in my living room. Come take them away!"

"'m *not* going to spend the rest of my life locked up in a cage somewhere! *No way!*" I leaped to my feet. "There's got to be a better answer!"

"I have them here," Dad said into the phone.

I glanced at Ben. He stood on his haunches with his powerful jaw wrapped around one of the cage bars. His fangs glistened with saliva as he chewed away at it.

I stared at his sharp, dripping fangs. Yes! That's it! I thought.

Suddenly, I knew the answer. Suddenly, I knew just what I had to do. I knew how to solve our problem.

I sprinted across the room.

I leaped at my father — and sank my teeth deep into his shoulder.

Startled, Dad dropped the phone.

Then he threw back his head — and howled in pain.

Lights in the neighboring houses flashed on — as the three of us ran through the night. Two wolf creatures and a dazed man.

Howling.

Running in the cool night air.

Running under the full moon . . .

Yes, I — Aaron Freidus — am a werewolf.

My father *used* to be a werewolf hunter. But not anymore. Now he's a werewolf too.

That's how I solved our problem. That's how I saved the day!

My dad used to think a werewolf lived in the woods outside our town. But he never found one. And everyone thought he was crazy. Including me.

But Dad isn't crazy — at least not anymore.

Because I have a feeling the woods outside our town are going to be crawling with werewolves.

I know it. I just know it.

About R.L. Stine

R.L. Stine is the most popular author in America. He is the creator of the *Goosebumps, Give Yourself Goosebumps, Fear Street*, and *Ghosts of Fear Street* series, among other popular books. He has written over 250 scary novels for kids. Bob lives in New York City with his wife, Jane, teenage son, Matt, and dog, Nadine.

Welcome to the new millennium of fear

Check out this
chilling preview of
what's next from
R.L. STINE

Horrors of the Black Ring

I stared deep into the ring. A cloudy form shifted inside the jewel. It moved as if — as if it were *alive*.

Miss Gold turned the ring in the light. The cloud became a face. It frowned inside the jewel.

I shuddered. It can't be a face! I thought. It looks so — so evil!

"What *is* that?" I gasped.

"It's a flaw in the jewel," Miss Gold explained. "A cloudy spot. And if you catch it in the right light, it looks like a face, doesn't it?"

I nodded. I couldn't take my eyes off the ring. The face inside it was so ugly. So creepy.

"Such a strange optical illusion," Miss Gold said, almost to herself. "Do you like it?"

I gulped. "Um, I guess so. I can't stop staring at it."

She smiled. "I know. I have the same problem."

"Where did you get the ring?" I asked.

"I found it in the school parking lot," she replied. "I thought I'd wear it until someone claims it."

"Has anyone claimed it yet?" I asked.

"No," she said. "And it's a good thing. Because the ring is stuck on my finger. I-I can't get it off."

She tugged on the ring, showing me. It stuck at her knuckle. "It's almost as if it shrank on my finger," she explained.

Miss Gold passed out the rest of the papers. My eyes kept going back to her ring.

She returned to the front of the room. "I know you're all getting ready for the spring carnival," she said. "You've got projects to make for the art sale. And the food committee has a lot of cooking to do. So" — she paused and grinned at us — "I'm not giving you any homework this weekend!"

We all cheered. Miss Gold is the greatest.

We settled down to study geography. Miss Gold pulled a map over to the chalkboard.

Her black ring flashed in the light. I kept thinking about the face in the jewel.

Sure, I thought, it's just some kind of smoky flaw. It only *looks* like a face.

It only *seems* to be moving.

So why is it so creepy?

Why can't I stop thinking about it?

3

"How could I be so stupid?" I grumbled. I tossed my paintbrush onto the table. I was trying to paint two hands clasped together — a symbol of brotherhood. But I forgot how hard it is to paint hands.

"I ask myself the same question every day," Anthony said. "'How could Beth be so stupid?'"

I glared at him but didn't say anything. He's so mean. And no matter what I say to him, he always gets the last word.

We were in the art room, working on our projects for the carnival art sale. I was in charge of the art sale. Danny was working on games and activities. Tina Crowley was organizing the food.

Everyone in the sixth grade was making something for the sale. I stared at my painting of lumpy, stumpy fingers and sighed. Nobody would want to buy *this* picture.

Anthony peeked over my shoulder. "That's great, Beth," he said. "What's it supposed to be? Why are those worms crawling over that sandwich?"

I could feel my face turning red. I glanced across the room at Danny Jacobs, to see if he'd heard. He was busy molding something out of clay.

Danny is so cute. He's got honey-brown hair, big brown eyes, and really long eyelashes. He's a little taller than I am, and very athletic. He's one of the best players on the soccer team.

"Or maybe you painted two *plants* shaking hands?" Anthony teased.

"If you're so great, let's see what *you're* painting," I replied.

He flashed me a mean grin. "You're going to love it!" he promised.

I stepped up to his easel and gasped. He was painting a round-faced girl with red hair and bulging, crossed eyes.

"Is that supposed to be me?" I cried.

"Ding ding ding! We have a winner!" he crowed. "You guessed right!"

I swallowed. The picture was really ugly. But I didn't want to let Anthony know it hurt me.

"I don't look like that," I sniffed. "Maybe if you took off your sunglasses you'd see me better."

Anthony tugged the dark glasses down his nose

and stared at me. "Nope — sorry," he said. "I can see better with my sunglasses on. It must be the glare bouncing off your pasty skin."

I opened my mouth to say something back — something good and mean. But the meanest thing I could think of was "Oh, yeah?"

I closed my mouth.

Someday I'll get him good, I fumed. If I could only think of a way. . . .

I decided to ignore him. I had no other choice. I glanced across the room at Danny. He was washing the clay off his hands.

Maybe this is my chance to talk to him, I thought. I crossed the room and stood beside him at the sink.

"Hi," I said.

He dried his hands. "Hi. How's your art project going?"

"Not so great," I admitted. I cleared my throat. "Um — do you think you could help me with something? I'm trying to paint hands, and I can't get the fingers right. Could I use your hands as a model?"

Danny nodded. "Sure. I'm waiting for my clay pot to dry, anyway."

He came over to the table and set his hands flat. "Like this?" he asked.

"That's good," I replied. I picked up my brush and started fixing up the worm fingers. I could feel Danny watching. It made me nervous. I had a hard time concentrating with him sitting right there.

What if he thinks my picture is lame? I thought.

"Oo, look at the lovebirds!" Anthony poked his head around his easel. He made juicy kissing noises. *SMACK, SMACK, SLUUURP.*

Oh, no, I thought. I should have known this would happen.

"Shut up, Gonzales," Danny snapped at him.

Nothing could make Anthony stop. "Beth is painting her true love. Can I come to the wedding?"

"Anthony — stop it!" I cried. He's ruining everything, I thought. Just as he always does.

Anthony puckered up and made the kissy sounds again.

Danny leaped to his feet. "You're looking for major trouble."

"Hey — watch out. I know karate!" Anthony shot back.

Danny threw himself at Anthony and knocked him to the floor. Anthony's sunglasses flew across the room.

"Danny — don't!" I pleaded.

They rolled around on the floor, kicking and punching and crashing into chairs.

"Hey, hey, HEY!" Mr. Martin, the art teacher, raced over to pull the boys apart. "What's going on here? Have you lost your minds?"

Anthony leaped up, wiping his nose. "He

jumped me. For no reason at all. He's crazy! He just attacked me!"

"Not true!" Danny protested. "He asked for it."

"All right, all right." Mr. Martin sighed. "Danny, go back over there where you were working before. Anthony, you stay here. Stay away from each other. And if I catch you fighting again, you're both going to the principal's office."

Danny frowned and went back to the clay table. Anthony leaned close to me and whispered, "Wave bye-bye to your boyfriend!"

"Anthony, you stink!" I muttered.

"Ouch! That hurt!" he teased.

I can't stand him.

He went back to the easel. He started painting very quickly, humming as he worked.

I knew he was adding to the ugly picture of me. I had to see what he was painting. I couldn't help myself.

I glanced at his paper. He was painting snot-colored drips running out of my nose.

"Like it?" he asked. "I was thinking of giving it to Danny. I know he'll want a picture of his girl-friend to hang inside his locker."

I hate him. I really hate him. Did I mention that?

After art class, Danny caught up with me in the hall. I was on my way to the cafeteria for lunch.

"Anthony is a total pain," Danny said. "He's always in my face."

"Mine too," I replied. I smiled. Maybe Anthony did me a favor after all. His bad jokes were bringing Danny and me together!

"Can I sit with you at lunch?" Danny asked me. "I'd like to tell you about some ideas I have for the carnival."

Yes! I thought. A little shiver of excitement shot through my skin. Stay cool, I told myself. Don't act too goofy.

"Sure," I said, trying to sound as if it was no big deal to sit next to the cutest boy in the class. "You know —"

A shrill scream interrupted me.

"Huh? What was that?" I gasped.

"It came from in there." Danny pointed to Miss Gold's room. We turned and burst into the classroom as another scream ripped through the air.

Miss Gold stood by the chalkboard, her face twisted in horror.

"What happened?" I cried. "What's wrong?"

Trembling, the teacher pointed to the chalkboard.

Every inch of it was covered with words. Someone had scrawled them over and over: THE CARNIVAL IS DOOMED. THE CARNIVAL IS DOOMED. THE CARNIVAL IS DOOMED.

"Wow," Danny gasped. "This is sick."

"Who did it?" I demanded.

Miss Gold's face crumpled, as if she were about to burst into tears. "I don't know!" she wailed. "I only left the room for a few minutes!"

Wow, I thought. Miss Gold is really upset.

I stared at the scribbled words. "Who would do this?"

"It's got to be a joke," Miss Gold murmured.

"What if it isn't a joke?" I asked. "What if somebody is serious about this?" Danny glanced at me. "What if someone is planning to do something horrible? Really horrible?"

Miss Gold shook her head. She didn't seem so upset anymore. "I don't think so. I'll bet someone is just trying to scare us a little."

"Well, anyway, we'll erase the chalkboard," I offered.

"Yeah," Danny agreed. "No problem."

"Thank you." Miss Gold sighed. "That's sweet of you guys."

I grabbed an eraser and tossed another one to Danny. We started to work erasing the scrawled words.

The carnival is doomed. The carnival is doomed.

The words repeated in my head, over and over. What did they mean?

Everybody loves the spring carnival, I thought. Why would anyone want to ruin it?

"Hey, guys, what's the word?" Anthony strolled into the room. "Playing teacher's pet again, Beth?"

"Somebody scribbled all over the chalkboard," Danny told him. "Want to help us?"

"Hey — I'd love to, but I can't." Anthony started to back out of the room. "I've got bad allergies, you know. Chalk dust makes me sneeze."

I stepped toward him, waving the chalky eraser. "Oh, yeah? Let's see."

Anthony held up his hands. "Really," he insisted. "I'm serious."

I stared at Anthony's hands.

Hey, wait, I thought.

Anthony's hands — they were covered with chalk dust.

5

-what are you looking at?" Anthony stammered, swinging his hands behind his back.

"Your hands are covered with chalk!" I accused.

Danny, Miss Gold, and I stared hard at him. He backed away.

"They — they are not!" he cried. "It isn't chalk — it's clay! I was helping Mr. Martin clean up after art class!"

"Yeah. Sure," Danny muttered. We both knew that helping teachers clean up is *not* the kind of thing Anthony Gonzales usually does.

"I've got to go," Anthony said. He hurried out of the room.

"He's got to go wash the evidence off his hands," Danny said.

"I'll bet Anthony did this," I replied. "He wanted to be in charge of the carnival. But no one wanted him."

"Yeah, I bet he's jealous," Danny agreed.

Miss Gold shook her head. "I can't believe Anthony would do this," she murmured. "The kids in this school are so nice. Nothing like this has ever happened here...."

But it *did* happen, I thought.

Somebody in this school is not so nice....

Amanda started driving me crazy as soon as I got up the next morning.

"Help me arrange my Barbies today!" she begged. "I want to line them all up in order — from prettiest to ugliest."

I sighed. "Amanda, all Barbies look exactly the same. One can't be prettier than another."

"That's not true! Surfer Barbie is beautiful, but Rollerblade Barbie is not so hot."

"Oh, please. Can't you do it yourself? I'm busy. I have to go to school today."

"Liar!" Amanda cried. "It's Saturday!"

"I know that," I replied. "I have carnival stuff to do."

Some of the kids hadn't finished their art projects for the carnival — including me. Also, I was in charge of the art sale, so I had to be there to help.

"But you promised!" Amanda cried.

"I did not!" I insisted. "You're such a liar."

"You're the liar!" she accused. "You never keep your promises, Beth Breath."

"That's because I never make them in the first place — Amanda Panda."

I hate it when she calls me Beth Breath. It sounds like I have bad breath or something — and I don't. And Amanda Panda just doesn't sound as bad.

"That stupid carnival takes up all your time. What about my cow eyeball?"

"Cow eyeball? What are you talking about?" I told you she was nuts.

"For my science class. The teacher said we could make up our own project. So I decided to dissect a cow eyeball. To see what's inside. And you said you'd help me!"

"Yuck. Where on earth did you get a cow eyeball?" I asked.

"I've had it in my room for a week. I got it from Teddy Jackson." Teddy Jackson is a boy in her class. His father works in some kind of lab. Teddy is always giving Amanda gross stuff to keep in her room.

"I can't believe you brought a real cow eyeball into the house," I said. "And you think *I'm* going to cut into it with a knife? You're crazier than I thought."

"You're crazy for liking Danny Jacobs!" she shot back.

"I don't like him!" I protested. "I'm sorry, Amanda, but I can't help you today. Maybe after the carnival is over."

"That will be too late!" Amanda started throwing one of her world-famous temper tantrums. "My project is due Monday!"

"I said I was sorry. There's nothing I can do about it."

"You'll be sorry, all right!" Amanda screeched. "Just wait and see!"

She slammed the door.

I hurried to the kitchen to find Mom. She always hides out in the kitchen when she hears me fighting with Amanda.

"Everything okay?" she asked when I stormed in.

"Why did you have to have another baby after me?" I demanded. "I would have been so happy as an only child."

Mom just shook her head. "Someday you'll be glad to have a sister."

I didn't think that day would ever come. But I kept my mouth shut. I had something else on my mind.

"Where's the bird?" I asked. "Did you take him to the vet?"

Mom nodded. "The vet put a splint on its wing. I bought a little cage for it on my way home. It's out on the back porch."

I went out to the porch. The little bird sat quietly in the cage. Mom had left him a pile of bird-seed. It didn't look as if he'd eaten much of it.

"How are you, little bird?" I cooed. "How's your broken wing?"

His wing was bandaged and it looked heavy. Poor little guy, I thought. He doesn't look too good.

I decided to name him Chirpy. I knew it was a stupid name. But I couldn't think of anything better.

I sat outside on the porch for a while. I thought it would be nice to keep Chirpy company.

After a while, Mom called me in to lunch. "How's the bird doing, honey?" she asked.

"Not so great," I answered.

"Maybe he'll be better tomorrow," Mom said. "Amanda, did you see Beth's bird?"

"She should have let Anthony run over it," Amanda muttered.

"How can you be so mean?" I demanded. "You and your cow eyeballs."

"I'm not speaking to you, Beth Breath," Amanda said.

"Good," I replied. "I don't want to hear anything you have to say, anyway."

"Girls —" Mom pleaded.

The rest of the lunch was pretty quiet. We talked to Mom. But we wouldn't talk to each other.

"I wish your father was here," Mom grumbled.

Dad was away on a business trip. "Every time he goes out of town, you girls start fighting."

After lunch I hurried to my room. I had to get ready to go to school.

As I grabbed my sweater, the phone rang. I have a phone in my room with my own separate line.

I picked it up. "Hello?"

"*Stay away,*" a strange voice whispered. The voice was muffled — as if someone were trying to disguise it.

"*Stay away. I'm warning you. Don't go to school today.*"

PREPARE TO BE SCARED!

Goosebumps® SERIES 2000
R.L. STINE

LOG ON FOR SCARE:

The latest books

Really gross recip

**Start your own
Goosebumps reading**

**How to get
Goosebumps stu
clothes, CD-ROM
video releases and**

**Author R.L. Stine
tips on writing!**

Goosebumps on the Wel

http://www.scholastic.com/Goosebum